DEDICATION

This book is dedicated to my most excellent friend, Pam Baillie, without whose encouragement I would not have considered publishing this collection. For good measure, she also proof-read it.

PREFACE

When the pandemic really began to take hold in the UK in early March 2020, I was working at the Cheltenham Racing Festival, an event that was controversial at the time, and which has been the subject of much debate ever since. I succumbed to the virus within days and was unwell for about two weeks from 16 March. Fortunately, I did not require medical treatment (and am therefore one of many who do not figure in the statistics!)

As I began to recover, I found that I had time and space to do things I don't normally do. In an idle moment, I decided to write a verse about the Government's "wash your hands" advice. Completely unexpectedly, this led me to continue churning out more songs, verses and satirical pieces almost on a daily basis. Some are humorous observations on the domestic consequences of lockdown and others about the politics and politicians involved. I need hardly add that Boris Johnson and Dominic Cummings figure prominently! These works comprise Part 1 of the collection.

But I have been writing limericks from time to time for many years, mostly to amuse myself. And, as a passionate pro-European, I was so devastated by the result of the Brexit Referendum (I still am!) that I consoled myself by writing satirical limericks about the characters involved – chiefly Theresa May and Boris Johnson – and about events as they unfolded; the fabled "Backstop" for instance. I have included them in Part 2, in chronological order, as the tortuous Brexit saga proceeded.

In summary, the collection forms a weird sort of historical record of these peculiar times. I hope you enjoy it.

MS

CONTENTS

Part 1 – The Lockdown

Part 1 (continued)

Mad Bad Dom
The Things Could Be Worse Verse
You Are Old, PM Boris

Part 2 – Brexit

A collection of Brexit-related limericks in
chronological order

Closing Thought

Silent letters

PART 1

THE LOCKDOWN

Wash Your Hands

This is my first composition, which can be sung to the tune of Ode for Joy (The anthem of the European Community!)

Wash your hands a lot more often
Twenty seconds at a time
Germs pose greater hidden dangers
Than the threat from muck and grime

Then maintain your social distance
Two whole metres from the next
You will thus delay the virus
And protect the NHS!

The Lockdown Cometh

(With thanks to Flanders and Swann for the inspiration. Their song, The Gasman Cometh, tells of a line of tradesmen who all cause some problem that another tradesman has to resolve the next day throughout the week until the gasman has to re-visit the following Monday. Look it up on YouTube)

'Twas on a Monday morning the lockdown was imposed
I stayed in bed all morning: in the afternoon I dozed,
In the evening I watched telly – such a lot I didn't like –
So I rummaged in the garden shed and found my rusty bike.

Oh, it all makes stuff for the locked-down chap to do!

'Twas on the Tuesday morning I hunted for some lube
But no amount of searching would reveal a single tube,
So I went and got the papers and read them end-to-end,
All that pious drivel nearly drove me round the bend.

Oh, it all makes stuff for the locked-down chap to do!

'Twas on the Wednesday morning, I thought I'd make a list
Of all the jobs I hadn't done – and some I hadn't wished:
There was tiling in the bathroom and painting in the hall,
Not to mention lots of garden, which I rarely touch at all.

Oh, it all makes stuff for the locked-down chap to do!

'Twas on the Thursday morning I started my first deed,
To make another list of all the items that I'd need,
But going to DIY shops all around the land,
As well as garden centres, was summarily banned.

Oh, it all makes stuff for the locked-down chap to do!

'Twas on the Friday morning I decided on a plan
To write a trendy novel about a locked-down man,
But sitting at the console just staring at the blighter
Quickly made me realise I wouldn't make a writer.

Oh, it all makes stuff for the locked-down chap to do!
On Saturday and Sunday I sat and watched it rain,
So 'twas on a Monday morning that I stayed in bed again!

Painting – A True Story

A bizarre postscript is that I actually decided to do some painting. Read on……

I had been looking at a water stain on the ceiling of my living room for several months and, having finally realised that it would not go away of its own accord, I decided that there was nothing to do but to paint it.

This was a momentous decision – I had never actually lifted a paintbrush in anger in my life. I had always regarded painting as a health and safety risk and therefore a job for professionals.

Anyway, ignoring these thoughts, I duly purchased the necessary paint and brushes. Of course, they then sat in the hall for another fortnight whilst I readied myself to do the actual deed (and wrote some more of this stuff).

I woke up on VE Day – also my 73rd Birthday – and decided this was the day!
At 07.30, I put the newspapers on the floor, got the step-ladder out of the shed, opened the paint tin, stirred the paint, put it on the platform of the ladder and began to climb. Unfortunately, the ladder – which had not been used for 20 years and was made of

wood – did not appreciate the burden I placed on it and one leg promptly collapsed. The paint tin overturned and spilled all over and through the inevitable gaps in the newspapers.

At 10.00, I had completed the clean-up operation and decided enough was enough for one day – especially on my birthday!

But undeterred, I purchased a (metal) step-ladder – and a new tin of paint – and commenced again the next morning. I did the necessary floor covering and started painting without any further alarms. After a while, I decided I needed to examine my handiwork, so I descended the ladder – paint tin in hand – took a step backwards and did a back-flip over a dining room chair which I had omitted to remove. The paint once more hit the floor and I spent another two hours cleaning up the mess. Pure Laurel and Hardy and a great shame that no-one else was there to enjoy the comedy routine!

I did eventually finish the project without too many further alarms but I concluded that this was to be a one-off experience. I had unwisely ignored the self-preservation instinct that had stopped me painting anything throughout my life. I will now stick to writing!

Nooks and Crannies

I wrote this early in the lockdown as a sort of mission statement to myself. Tune - Cwm Rhondda (Bread of Heaven)

In the lockdown, what do you do
With your time by day and night?
Imagination at a standstill?
Just clean everything in sight!

Nooks and crannies, nooks and crannies,
Clean from ceiling to the floor,
Clean from ceiling to the floor.

Soap and water at the ready,
Dusters, hoovers and the like.
Rub and polish with a vigour,
Curtains to all bugs and mites!

Nooks and crannies, nooks and crannies,
Wash the windows and the doors,
Wash the windows and the doors.

Change the bedclothes, bleach the toilet,
Not forgetting sinks and drains.
Buff the woodwork, dust the sofa,
Then do everything again!

Nooks and crannies, nooks and crannies,
Clean the house for evermore,
Clean the house for evermore!

Heir? – Apparently!

The Prime Minister, Boris Johnson, caught the virus and was absent for several weeks. The Foreign Secretary, Dominic Raab, stood in as his designated deputy. This is an imagined story of his reaction.

The First Secretary of State awoke suddenly in a cold sweat. He had been in the middle of a dream which had started pleasantly enough but had turned darker as it proceeded. He had been walking through a delightful country village, listening to the distant roar of trucks on the motorway across the fields thundering their way back and forth to the coast. In the dream, he was idly conjecturing why so much trade still needed to go through Dover, Brexit having happened two months before, when his thoughts were brought sharply into the present by the sound of the bells of the parish church. Dim-Dom, Dim-Dom, Dim-Dom they seemed to be saying. He knew this was the cruel nickname by which he was known in the Foreign Office. Normally, he ignored it - a thick skin being a pre-requisite for any minister of the Crown - but now it served to reinforce his own misgivings about the role into which he had so cruelly been thrust.

He knew deep down that the PM had probably made him First Secretary of State because he would be no kind of threat to him but now that he had to perform the role, he could see nothing but difficulties. If he appeared too competent and authoritative, he would generate jealousies from within the ambitious cabal led by the Oily Gove and the depressingly impressive new Chancellor. He would have added Hancock to the list but he thought it possible that he had already had his half-hour! He smiled grimly at his own joke and continued to wrestle with his dilemma. In these circumstances, he would also undoubtedly incur the displeasure of the PM who would inevitably demote him at the first opportunity. Of course, if he did not display competence and authority he would be a goner anyway. This was the ultimate lose-lose situation. In desperation, he decided there was nothing to lose by confiding his misgivings to his wife.

After listening to his delirious babble, she said nothing. Instead, she got silently out of bed, went into the bathroom and brought back a thermometer. "Stick this in your gob", she said. "Add two to any reading you get, ring Downing Street in the morning and self-isolate for fourteen days. Goodnight!"

The Rhyme Of The Lockdown 2020 (1)

*When I heard the news that the Chief
Medical Officer for Scotland – Dr Clare
Calderwood – had ignored her own
lockdown advice and travelled to her
weekend home in Fife (twice!), I decided that
it was time to attempt a McGonagall-type
poem.*

'Twas in the visionary year of 2020
When we had been promised riches aplenty
That the dreaded coronavirus
Came along and tried to expire us.
But we locked down with determination
In a bid to save the nation.
The PM took one for the team,
And hasn't for some time been seen.
So we had the pleasure of Michael Gove
Instructing on how we shouldn't rove,

And then a medic north of the border,
Perhaps in remembrance of Harry Lauder,
Took non-essential travel advice
In person - all the way to Fife.
Not quite the Tay Bridge Disaster
But it caused much unkind laughter.
This noble act being unappreciated
She sensibly self-decapitated.

Down south Her Majesty has stated
That the World War II spirit should be re-
created,
And good old Vera Lynn - she won't drop
We'll Meet Again is still Top of the Pops!

Captain Tom Moore

*Captain Tom Moore became an instant
celebrity by walking around his garden to
raise money to support the NHS. He initially
hoped to raise £1,000 but the final total was
£33 million. This is my tribute to him.*

A Hero of The Lockdown

Near Bedford, good old Captain Tom
Walked round his garden, on and on,
He just said "I'll do my bit –
Why shouldn't I? I'm fighting fit!"
As his 100th birthday neared,
Naturally the people feared
He would be "Run-out, 99",
Like Atherton at Lords that time.
But anxious we should not have been –
He managed it: his style serene.
Top of the Pops and a promotion,
Many cards and much commotion,
With campaign medals on his chest
Raised millions for the NHS!

50 Things To Do Before You Die (Lockdown Version)

Forget Niagara Falls, a trip to The Serengeti or white-water rafting in New Zealand, you need something more attainable in the current circumstances;-

1. Wake-up
2. Get out of bed
3. Bowel movement
4. Shower
5. Shave/apply make-up
6. Make bed
7. Get dressed
8. Comb/brush hair
9. Buy newspaper
10. Have breakfast
11. Wash-up breakfast dishes
12. Tidy-up
13. Sort recyclables
14. Dust
15. Vacuum
16. Polish
17. Food shopping
18. Coffee and biscuits
19. Crossword
20. Sudoku
21. Read magazine
22. Gardening
23. Read emails
24. Check Facebook

25. Prepare lunch
26. Eat lunch
27. Wash-up lunch dishes
28. Snooze
29. Listen to radio
30. Reply to emails
31. Post on Facebook
32. Read text messages
33. Reply to text messages
34. Watch Government Press Conference (optional)
35. Tea and cake
36. Go for walk
37. G & T (or substitute)
38. Urinate (if not done earlier)
39. Chat on telephone
40. Prepare supper
41. Eat supper
42. Glass of wine/beer
43. Wash-up supper dishes
44. Watch telly
45. Bedtime drink
46. Clean teeth
47. Go to bed
48. Read book
49. Have sex (optional)
50. Sleep

Slimericks

Actually Clerihews – named after Edmund Clerihew Bentley who is credited with using this format first. But I prefer to call them Slimericks – 4 lines instead of 5.

Boris Johnson (1)

Our P.M., Boris Johnson
Has seldom, if ever, done
A very hard day's grafting
He much prefers a bit of shafting!

Boris Johnson (2)

Johnson, Alexander Boris de Pffefel,
Doesn't go in for a kiss and a tell.
He prefers to keep schtum about past assignations
In case they prompt some reciprocations!

Robert Jenrick

Robert Jenrick is S of S Communities
But changes homes with impudent impunity.
One day it's here, the next it's there,
He moves around without a care!

Jeremy Corbyn

Labour Party Ex-Leader Corbyn
Was definitely not very absorbing.
He came and he went without a win.
Let's hope he hasn't got a twin!

George Eustice

George Eustice is in charge of Environment,
A man whose name is heaven-sent
For limerick and wicked rhyme,
But do I really have the time?

Rishi Sunak

Chancellor of the Exchequer, Sunak,
Has developed a most clever knack.
He spends zillions of pounds
Without saying where it can be found!

Priti Patel

Home Secretary, Priti Patel,
Doesn't read numbers too well.
Forty hundred, two thousand and three
Doesn't sound quite right to me!

Professor Ferguson

The man who produced the mathematical model which persuaded Government to lockdown and then ignored his own advice by arranging trysts with his lover

When a mathematician of renown
Said we really have to lock down,
He forgot to estimate the chance
of being caught without his pants!

At Professor Ferguson's insistence
We had to keep our social distance,
But maths and hormones don't quite fit
And he was caught for doing his bit!
(in a manner of speaking)

Multiple Choice Question

Does PPE stand for :-

A. Pass Parcel Endlessly

B. Please Procrastinate Effectively

C. Pretty Poor Execution

(Answer – A, B and C)

Jerusalem In Lockdown

Early in the Lockdown, Derbyshire Police were accused of being a little "over-zealous" in their application of the Lockdown Rules. I decided that it needed properly "celebrating" in song.

And did those feet in Lockdown times
Walk upon England's mountains green?
And was a woman with her dog
On England's pleasant pastures seen?
And did a rambler on his own
Stride forth upon our clouded hills?
Or were they clobbered, all of them,
By chaps from Derbyshire Old Bill?

Bring me my notebook and my pen,
Bring me my taser and my gun,
Bring me my little panda car,
Bring me my hat and uniform.
I will not leave a stone unturned
And will make sure all byelaws stand
Till we have locked down everyone
In England's green and pleasant land.

Westminster Strollers X1 - Mid-Season Report

I wrote this in early May after watching Cabinet members taking their turns to host the daily press briefings which became such a feature of our daily lives. The PM was in hospital with the virus during most of this period.

Despite wonderful early-season weather, the team has failed to hit full stride. Sticking together manfully in the enforced absence of the captain but failing to inspire the watchers. Weaknesses in many positions becoming increasingly evident. Player profiles (in batting order):-

1. Raab (Vice-Captain) - Shouldered the burden of captaincy in Johnson's absence early in the season without complaint or, sad to say, notable success. Tends to be a bit tentative and defensive, especially early in the innings. But when he gets going, he can suddenly change pace and verge on recklessness.

2. Jenrick - Batting tends to be a bit robotic and often gives the appearance of solidity without delivering a big innings. Energetic in the field: tends to change position a lot without waiting for instruction from the

Captain. Dropped one absolute sitter recently.

3. Sunak - The new star of the team. Promoted from the 2rd X1 in an emergency, he has played something of a blinder so far - flashing strokes all around the field. It remains to be seen whether he can build on an encouraging start.

4. Johnson (Captain) - Missed early part of season. Passing resemblance to Flintoff but possibly more of a Botham-type - especially off the field. Doesn't like to be tied down and pulls off some imaginative strokes. A good "slipper".

5. Hancock (Wicket-keeper) - Required to do much of the hard graft after failures by top order. Handles all situations enthusiastically and attacks at all times, possibly because defence is not too sound. Drops the odd chance behind the stumps but never let it bother him (until recently).

6. Eustice - Lacks experience. Batting a bit agricultural. Often caught at cow corner.

7. Gove - Spinner. Has developed a new delivery called a "porkie". Talks constantly when fielding at slip to irritate opposition.

8. Wallace - Bowler. Can send down some deadly missiles. Stout defence when batting.

9. Shapps - Bowls with boyish enthusiasm, but too many wides. In and out of the team.

10. Sharma - Not clear why he is in the team. Stonewalls adequately without scoring many.

11. Patel - Making up the numbers.

12th Man - Rees-Mogg - Only used in an emergency. Has not adjusted well to the demands of modern-day game.

Next Match v Media. 5.00 at The Lecterns

The Rhyme of the Lockdown 2020 (2)

After McGonagall (again)

Meanwhile, our PM lay in intensive care –
And the nation held its breath to see how he
would fare.
While he was, at times, almost mortally
unwell,
His underlings were unimpressing, truth to
tell.
The location of Jenrick's main residence
caused quite a kerfuffle,
He has survived for now but will be wary of
the next re-shuffle

In PM's absence, Raab, Deputy Head Boy,
Was given the reins, to Gove's evident
disjoy.
His great talent for adequacy shone through
And he is still holding the reins even noo.
Jenrick (again) told us a plane from Istanbul
Would fly into Heathrow very full
Of PPE for all the NHS,
But what arrived was late – and sadly
useless!

Then the PM's girlfriend had a bairn,
Which gave Boris the excuse to avoid his
turn
To face new Labour leader, Starmer QC
Who will undoubtedly grill him forensically.

Returning north of the border,
Facemasks seem to be in order
Or, at least, that is the strong advice
Because breathing on your neighbour is nae
nice.
Down south Matt Hancock somehow met
His target for the end of April tests.

At home, having bought up all the flour,
Folks are baking more and more.
And gardening has come back on trend
As trendy people say in the West End.
Then PM Boris had an unconvincing return
To the press briefing lectern.
His bounce was clearly not the same,
Perhaps he's passed it onto baby
whathisname?

Offstage, Professor Lockdown from Imperial
College,
The man with the mathematical knowledge,
Has failed to follow his own SAGE advice
And is no longer a model for the populace.

50 More Things To Do Before You Die (Still Locked-Down version)

1. Fold pyjamas neatly
2. Scratch ass
3. Cut nails
4. Pick nose
5. Clean ears
6. Floss teeth
7. Put all household equipment instructions in one place
8. Wash inside of swing bin
9. Re-arrange food cupboards
10. Check use-by dates and deal accordingly
11. Clean cutlery
12. Wash kitchen floor
13. Sew holes in pockets
14. Sort shed contents
15. Check clothes for moth holes
16. Check that all pens still write
17. Throw out old telephone directories
18. Read junk mail
19. Watch Youtube
20. Listen to music
21. Watch daytime TV (not recommended)
22. Write will
23. Bake a cake
24. Put books in sensible order
25. Remove ones to go to charity shop
26. Examine contents of drawers

27. Remove all old shoelaces and random string
28. Sort clothes to go to charity shop
29. Watch Netflix
30. Write a letter to someone with a pen
31. Check all prints and paintings with spirit level
32. Clean spectacles
33. Sort Christmas decorations
34. Revise Christmas card list
35. Write Christmas cards (if you have them)
36. Meditate
37. Exercise
38. Dance
39. Sing
40. Sort tie drawer
41. Cut the grass
42. Polish shoes
43. Clean windows
44. Write a verse or two
45. Check bathroom cabinet and throw out old medicines
46. Read the meters
47. Check bank statement
48. Sort old photos
49. Read this rubbish
50. Get drunk

Lines to Celebrate the Birth of the PM's Son

Rejoice! A Boris bouncing baby boy
Is born this week to bring him joy.
Will he have the tousled hair,
The pudgy face, the pleading stare?
Will he rise to replicate
His pater's current high estate?
All will be revealed anon, anon:
Let's just pray he doesn't Carrie on!

Disinfecting Donald

*Donald Trump exceeded his own capacity
for idiocy by suggesting that people might
inject themselves with disinfectant to kill the
virus. This is a logical extension of the
suggestion. Don't try this at home!*

When Donald's been on the job
And his todger is starting to throb,
He doesn't get queasy
The answer's quite easy –
He puts some bleach on his knob!

Jacob Rees-Mogg

*The Leader of the House, whose speciality
seems to be turning the clock back*

Listening to Jacob Rees-Mogg
Can produce intellectual fog
So tune in instead
Just before bed
And you'll find you sleep like a log!

Pandemic Xmas Cracker Joke (29/04/20)

Q. What face-covering does a Scotsman
wear during a pandemic?

A. A Maskintosh

Staying Alert

*After 8 weeks in which the Government's
core message was Stay at Home", it
changed to "Stay Alert" which served only to
confuse people and caused much derision.
Anything to help!*

The housemaid said, "While I iron your shirt,
By Jove I'll be staying alert"

The gardener said, "I'm not digging much dirt
But, by Heaven, I'm staying alert"

The journalist said, "I'm digging the dirt
To check who is staying alert"

My girlfriend said "You'd better not flirt.
I will know cos I'm staying alert"

An old man said, "Help me, I'm hurt
I should have been staying alert"

The policeman, in tones which were curt,
Said "You're nicked for not staying alert"

Dominic Cummings

*Towards the end of May, there was a week
of huge furore after it had been discovered
that the PM's Chief Adviser, Dominic
Cummings, had visited Durham with his
family during the Lockdown in apparent
breach of Government Guidelines - which he
had helped to draft!*

The PM's Chief Adviser
Ought to have been wiser
You don't get off the hook
By cocking such a snook!

(I appear to have been wrong on this one!)

The Man who Broke the Rules in Barnard Castle

(Tune: *The Man who Broke the Bank at Monte Carlo*)

As I stroll along the River Tees with an
independent air
You can hear the folks declare
Should he really be up there?
You can see them faint and start to die
But I just turn and wink an eye
I'm the man who broke the rules in Barnard
Castle.

Addition to English Dictionary

Eyesight-seeing – The action of testing
eyesight by visiting a tourist attraction.

Is this the way to Barnard Castle

When the day is dawning
On Easter Sunday morning,
How I long to be there
Just to see if I can see there.
Never mind the Guidelines
That's not where I'm at,
It's my partner's birthday
So I can't stop to chat.

Is this the way to Barnard Castle
I want to get there with no hassle,
Dreaming dreams of Barnard Castle
And River Tees that lovely beck.
Show me the way to Barnard Castle
I'm not really such an asshole,
Lying over Barnard Castle
Is just a way to save my neck.

Sha la la la la la la
Sha la la la la la la
Sha la la la la la la
And sweet Mary who writes with me

Now it's slowly dawning
That my trip last Sunday morning,
Might scupper my career
If I don't make it clear –
It was a valid journey
That I took to see
If I could find the highway,

Then they might leave me be.

Is this the way to Barnard Castle
I need to get there with no hassle,
Dreaming dreams of Barnard Castle
And sweet Mary who writes for me.
Show me the way from Barnard Castle
It's been nothing but a hassle
Crying over Barnard Castle
And sweet Mary who came with me

Sha la la la la la la
Sha la la la la la la
Sha la la la la la la
And sweet Mary who came with me

Mad Bad Dom

Inspired by Big Bad John, a country and western hit in 1961 for Jimmy Dean

Every morning at nine you could see him arrive
He stood five foot six and weighed one forty five
Kinda narrow at the shoulder and bald at the tip
Everybody knew you didn't give no lip to Mad Dom

Mad Dom, Mad Dom, Mad Bad Dom

Nobody knew where Dom called home
It might be Durham or Camden Town
He didn't say much, kinda quiet and dry
If you spoke at all, you just said "Hi" to Mad Dom
Somebody called him Swiss Cottage Svengali
But he got marched out into the alley
And a torrent of oaths as he lay on the floor
Was Dom's way of saying "Don't mess no more, with Mad Dom"

Mad Dom, Mad Dom, Mad Bad Dom

Then came the day when the roof fell in
The papers found out where he'd been
Staying in Durham in the Lockdown
When he really should have stayed in town
All round the land there were calls for his head
But he just gave a shrug and said
"I'm not moving – that's for certain
Cos you ain't got no serious dirt on, Mad Dom"

Mad Dom, Mad Dom, Mad Bad Dom

So the press went away from Downing Street
Their moral win turned to defeat
And now the Adviser-in-Chief lives on
Nobody messes with Mad Bad Dom

Mad Dom, Mad Dom, Mad Bad Dom

Meanwhile, in the USA……..

<u>The Things Could Be Worse Verse</u>

Whenever you're tempted to say,
"Things aren't too spiffing today",
Whatever you care for
Do not despair for –
You're not in Trump's USA!

When you're fed up with the fray,
And your favourite cat's gone astray,
Refuse to give in,
And pour a big gin –
You're not in Trump's USA!

If the bills just won't go away
And the dog has refused to obey,
You'll be tempted to curse,
But things could be worse –
You're not in Trump's USA!

When play-station refuses to play,
And your supper slips off the tray,
Don't stamp your feet
Just simply repeat –
I'm not in Trump's USA!

You Are Old, PM Boris

We live in times when the remarkable has become commonplace - a world which Lewis Carroll would have relished. When a young, black, working-class footballer can run rings around a middle-aged, white, Old Etonian Prime Minister and, with quiet dignity, force a U-turn in Government policy without anyone seeming very surprised, you know we are in a very strange place. The episode brought to mind Carroll's famous poem "You are old, Father William"

"You are old PM Boris," the young striker said,
"And your hair has become very white;
And yet you incessantly stand on your head
Do you think at your age it is right?"

"In my youth," PM Boris replied to the lad
"I feared it would injure my brain
But now that I'm perfectly sure I have none
Why, I do it again and again!"

"You are old," said the youth, "as I mentioned before,
And have grown most uncommonly fat
Yet you do U-turns - at least 3 or 4 –
Pray what is the reason for that?"

"In my youth," said the toff, as he shook his thatched locks,
"I abandoned a principled stand
So nothing I now do is really a shock
But I'm sure you won't understand!"

"You are old," said young Marcus; "your contours are iffy;
You clearly eat too much suet
And can finish a bottle of plonk in a jiffy
Pray how do you manage to do it?"

"In my youth," said the toff, "I was taught how to drink
By my chums in the Bullingdon Club
And the lessons I learned then I think
Have enormously helped me to glug"

"You are old," said the youth, "one would hardly suppose
That untruths would pass your lips ever
But you do so without any growth of your nose:
What made you so awfully clever?"

"I have answered three questions, and that is enough,"
Said the toff, "Remember your station:
Do you think I can listen all day to such stuff?
Don't forget that I still run the nation!"

PART 2

THE BREXIT LIMERICKS

<u>Customs Concerns (10/05/18)</u>

When you first berth in S Creek
With perishable goods that you seek
To land in a day
They will say "Go away -
Can you come back next week?"

<u>Brexit Mess (25/05/18)</u>

I've decided it's time I began
Not picturing worms in a can
So inside my head
I've replaced it instead
With an image of stuff hitting fan!

<u>Fudge(08/06/18)</u>

Though forcibly given a nudge
Theresa PM will not budge.
She may not or she may
Decide something one day,
Or she might be addicted to fudge!

The Death of Lord Carrington (10/07/18)

A distinguished former Foreign Secretary in Mrs Thatcher's Government, who resigned when Argentina invaded the Falkland Islands, though many, including Mrs Thatcher, felt he didn't need to. An old-school statesman!

Lord Carrington waited to go
Until Johnson left the F.O.
He rests in peace
Knowing Boris has ceased
Turning statesmanship into a show!

The D.U.P (12/10/18).

The position of the DUP:
"No border in the Irish Sea" –
Is very fraught
And prompts this thought –
Do headless chickens pass for free?

The Backstop (18/10/18)

Boris says "It isn't cricket",
Arlene tells 'em where to stick it,
But Theresa has a plan
Hitherto unknown to man –
She'll move backstop to deep midwicket!

I'm Off (30/10/18)

There once was a thing called Brexit
Which nobody knew how to fit
Into a plan
Before it hit pan
So I think I'll become an Ex-Brit!

A Brief Escape (20/11/18

A week golfing in Fuerteventura
Might not make me holy or purer
But leaving UK
On Brexithog Day
Will certainly help - nothing surer!

MAYDAY (15/12/18)

Whatever Theresa might say
I simply can't see a way
Out of this mess
With any success
MAYhem, then MAYDAY, MAYDAY!

Corbyn (28/12/18)

Jezza's still Leader of Labour
Which isn't a prospect to savour
For God's sake – Resign
While there's still time
And do us all a big favour!

Rees-Mogg (28/12/18)

Said Jacob to Mrs Rees-Mogg
Whenever you sit on the bog
Start quoting Virgil
You'll find that the urge'll
Start to make things unclog!"

Trump (07/01/19)

I'm President Donald J Fuck
And when I find that I'm stuck,
I tweet constant crap
Without taking the rap
Then drop someone else in the muck!

Bercow (07/01/19)

Have you noticed that Speaker Bercow
Has a name that sounds like "Berk Go"
By nature, by name,
So if it's all the same
We think you should say "Cheerio"!

Plan B (24/01/19)

When Theresa unveiled Plan B
There wasn't a change I could see
But closer inspection
Revealed this correction -
Groundhogs get in for free!

The Bridgwater Camel (21/01/19)

There was a papier mache camel standing in a field looking over the M5 for many years. It was an old friend who I nodded to on my frequent journeys to Devon. It disappeared a couple of years ago and then reappeared for a time. Sadly, it now seems to have gone for good.

Even when things look so black
There's always some light through the crack,
So forget Mrs May
If just for today –
The Bridgwater Camel is back!

The Indefinite Article (18/02/19)

It has only just to me occurred
That MAY's an indefinite word,
So making Theresa
Our Country's leader
Was clearly deeply absurd!

Distillation Process (08/03/19)

When Theresa distils her position
She may well find that her mission
To cobble a brew
Will appeal to so few
That the EU will hoot with derision!

May v May (21/03/19)
Erskine May - Parliamentary Rule Book

Theresa wants a replay
But Erskine is barring her way
The Speaker has stated
It can't be debated
So now it is May versus May!

Jeremy Corbyn's Pledge(24/03/19)

This is my sincere dedication
That I solemnly pledge to the nation –
A firm policy
Of wait…. and then see
Let's call it "Clear Obfuscation"!

Theresa Endgame (24/05/19)

What will happen today
Is really not easy to say,
A look at the date
Could foretell her fate –
It's nearly the end of May!

Transition(24/07/19)

It's goodbye to Tainted Theresa
And hello Etonian Geezer
A man with no morals
Is taking the laurels -
It's Boris, the modern-day Caesar!

CLOSING THOUGHT

I came across a Victorian spelling book recently. In the chapter on "silent letters", it gives many examples, of which the first is "The Premier has been arraigned for high treason, and consigned to the Tower"!

Printed in Great Britain
by Amazon